Pierre in Love

BY **SARA PENNYPACKER**   PICTURES BY **PETRA MATHERS**

ORCHARD BOOKS   NEW YORK   AN IMPRINT OF SCHOLASTIC INC.

Pierre was in love.

He had all the symptoms. He stared into space for hours on end. He tossed and turned all night, and deep plum-colored shadows had grown beneath his eyes.

He could not eat; his favorite chowder tasted like paste, and cheeses he had once loved lay in his mouth like stones. His face melted into a loopy smile whenever he heard her name — Catherine! — or even a word that sounded like Catherine: *aspirin* for example, or *bathroom*.

How he longed to speak to her, to tell her how he felt!

Pierre sighed tragically — this was exactly what he could not do. Catherine was exquisite, an angel of grace and beauty, and he was only an ordinary fisherman.

In the mornings, steaming out, he passed her studio. He saw her teaching ballet to the children who lived in town. He heard her voice: *Plié, mes enfants, plié!* floating like a silver ribbon over the harbor. And his heart beat so loudly it drowned out the engine of his boat.

In the evenings, pulling back into port, he saw
her painting at an easel. *How elegant she was!*
he marveled. *How clean! How . . . how unlike
himself.*

Pierre sighed another tragic sigh and began to pull in his lines, the final haul of the day. Some clams, three lobsters, a single bass. The blue scales reminded him of how much he wanted to speak to Catherine. Of course, everything reminded him of this: sunrises, sunsets, empty potato chip bags.

And then there, tangled at the end of his line, was an unbroken shell, as perfect in its beauty as Catherine herself!

He would give it to her — he must! — as a token of
the love he could not express in words. Perhaps she would
paint it; how happy that would make her! Pierre hoisted his
anchor — tonight it seemed as light as a gull feather — and
turned his boat toward the harbor.

In his cottage, Pierre washed the shell with great care. Then he tied a ribbon around it. It was ready!

After an extra-long shower, Pierre combed his hair back and styled his mustache with squid ink. He polished his teeth. He tried on everything in his closet and finally selected a dashing red silk shirt — red, he knew, was the color of love. He inspected himself in the mirror, then stepped back to get the full picture. Perfect! He did not look a bit like the fisherman he had been just an hour ago!

He flew out the door and down the road to Catherine's studio. His heart surged as wild as a hurricane sea as he raised his hand to knock on her door.

Then he froze.

What had he been thinking? What would he say when she came to the door?

Pierre laid the shell on Catherine's doorstep, and fled.

The next morning, Catherine rose early and went outside to perform some stretches, as usual. Her heart gave a *petit jeté* when she saw Pierre's gift.

"Oh, how lovely!" she cried. "But who could have left it?"

All that day Miss Catherine's students wondered what was making their teacher smile in such a mysterious way.

Miles out at sea, Pierre was smiling, too. As he fished, his thoughts flew to Catherine's studio. Was she holding the shell at this very moment, admiring its beauty? His heart swelled with its secret.

Pierre baited his hooks and allowed himself to daydream further. In his imagination, Catherine was in some sort of grave danger and he would swoop in and rescue her in the nick of time.

"Oh, how can I ever thank you?" she would exclaim when she was recovered enough to speak. "You saved my life!"

Then Pierre would shrug modestly — he practiced this shrug so he would be ready — and brush off her gratitude.

"Not at all," he would say in a voice quite a bit deeper than his regular one. "It was nothing. The important thing is that you are all right."

But after a while, his daydreams were not enough.

Ahead, Pierre saw a small island covered with wild roses. He anchored his boat, swam ashore, and collected an enormous bouquet — at great risk to himself, for the roses were thorny.

He would give the flowers to Catherine! And this time, he vowed, he would hand them to her and stay to speak to her!

Once again, he cleaned and polished himself until he shone in his red, red shirt. But once again, fear seized him at Catherine's doorstep, and he laid the bouquet down and fled.

And once again, when Catherine opened the door the next morning and saw Pierre's gift, she wondered who had left it and her heart leaped a *petit jeté*.

The next morning, a piece of driftwood appeared on her doorstep.

The next, a heart-shaped wreath of sea grass.

And the next, a dozen oysters in a bucket of ice.

Catherine could bear the suspense no longer. That night, she hid in the lilac bushes beside her door, and chewed on fiery cinnamon candies to stay awake.

At midnight, Pierre crept to Catherine's door and bent to arrange a pile of sea-smoothed stones.

He heard a noise, and whirled around to see Catherine leap gracefully from a bush.

"So it was you, sir!" she cried. "You've been leaving me these gifts!"

Pierre was so stunned he could only stare, his mouth hanging open like a haddock's. This close to Catherine, he felt all bloopy and love-swoggled.

But it was now or never.

"I love you," he burst out, "and my deepest wish is that you could love me, too."

"The gifts are beautiful, sir," Catherine replied. "But I cannot love you. I'm in love with someone else already."

Pierre staggered. The news socked him hard, like an anchor to his chest.

"Well," he said, struggling to smile, "I'm glad to know you are happy."

"Oh," Catherine said with a mournful shrug, "I'm not happy. I can't eat; I can't sleep. I love him, but I've never even met him. I can't tell him how I feel because he's an adventurer, bold and brave, and I'm only an ordinary ballet teacher. All I can do is paint pictures of him, and so I do, night after night."

Pierre couldn't take any more. He ran to his cottage and wept like a broken wave.

But the next morning, he felt a little better. For the first time in months he had slept well, and he had managed a few bites of oatmeal for breakfast. It wasn't being in love that had made him so miserable, he realized. It was keeping it a secret.

Pierre picked up the dashing red shirt from the floor. It was still sopping wet from his tears, but he would tie it to his mast to dry in the sun. His heart was mending already.

On the way to the dock, he suddenly turned and ran to Catherine's studio — he had one more gift to give her.

"Tell him!" Pierre called out, as loud as he could. "Feelings are like tides — you can't hold them back!" Before Catherine could open the door, he spun away and raced to the dock.

That day, the sunlight sparkled like diamonds on the waves, and the fish practically flung themselves into his nets. Pierre tried to enjoy himself. *I have a finest-kind boat,* he reflected, *a snug home, and excellent health. So what if I have no one to share it all with?*

"I'm as happy as a clam on the lam!" he sang out loud every time he caught himself wondering if this were the moment Catherine was telling her beloved how she felt. And by the time he reached the harbor, he almost believed it.

There in the distance was his dock. But something about it looked different tonight! Drawing closer, Pierre was astonished to see that the pilings were hung with dozens of paintings.

And tying up to the dock, he saw something more astonishing still: The paintings were all of him, guiding his boat into port!

Just then, Catherine stepped out from behind the largest painting.

"I love you," she began, "And my deepest wish is that . . ."

She stopped. She stared at the red silk shirt flying from the hoisting pole. She rubbed her eyes and looked at Pierre. "*It's you!*" she cried, dumbfounded. "I almost didn't recognize you. . . ."

And then she stopped again, for really, what more was there to say?

Catherine and Pierre

flew into each other's embrace. Her heart gave a
grand jeté and his surged as wild as a hurricane sea . . .
or was it the other way around? It was impossible to tell
because their two hearts had become one.

For Pella, who taught us all about love.

—S.P.

To Gero and Linane

—P.M.

Text copyright © 2007 by Sara Pennypacker

Illustrations copyright © 2007 by Petra Mathers

All rights reserved. Published by Orchard Books, an imprint of Scholastic Inc., *Publishers since 1920.* ORCHARD BOOKS and design are registered trademarks of Watts Publishing Group, Ltd., used under license. SCHOLASTIC and associated logos are trademarks and/or registered trademarks of Scholastic Inc. No part of this publication may be reproduced, stored in a retrieval system, or transmitted in any form or by any means, electronic, mechanical, photocopying, recording, or otherwise, without written permission of the publisher. For information regarding permission, write to Orchard Books, Scholastic Inc., Permissions Department, 557 Broadway, New York, NY 10012.

Library of Congress Cataloging-in-Publication Data

Pennypacker, Sara, 1951-Pierre in love / by Sara Pennypacker; illustrations by Petra Mathers. —1st ed.   p. cm.
Summary: Feeling "bloopy and love-swoggled" in the presence of Catherine, the elegant ballet teacher, a humble fisherman tries to muster the courage to reveal his affection for her. ISBN-13: 978-0-439-51740-9 ISBN-10: 0-439-51740-0 [1. Love—Fiction. 2. Honesty—Fiction. 3. Fishers—Fiction.] I. Mathers, Petra, ill. II. Title. PZ7.P3856Pi 2007 [E]—dc22 2006017543   10 9 8 7 6 5 4 3 2 1   07 08 09 10 11
Printed in Singapore 46   First edition, January 2007

The art was created with watercolor on Arches 300# cold press.
The display type is set in House Cut. The text type is ITCSouvenir Light.